To Tasha, whose love of nature
made this story possible.
M.C.

To my mother, Jean Broda.
Love, Number Six
R.B.

Out beyond the town, where the farms begin, is an unusual field. In the early spring, when all the other fields are bare and brown, this field is green and bright because it is filled with little Christmas trees. This is the story of one special tree.

From where the little tree was growing, among the rows and rows of trees, he could at last see the big, bold letters of the sign that had puzzled him for so long. There it stood, at the end of the field — "Brown's Christmas Tree Farm."

He was sure that he was a tree, but he didn't know what a Christmas tree was, or even what Christmas was. He did know that he was supposed to grow straight and tall and healthy for some special reason.

Every few days a man would walk past and look at him. The man would pull out the weeds around his trunk and spray him all over, getting rid of the itchy bugs and the pesky caterpillars that clogged up his needles and nibbled at his bark.

By the time he was seven years old, the little tree was big enough for birds and other creatures to perch on his branches. He looked forward to the arrival of such new visitors in the hope that they would be able to answer his questions about Christmas.

His first visitor was a goose, who stopped to nibble the fresh young grass by his trunk. "Please, Miss Goose," asked the tree, "what is Christmas? And what is a Christmas tree?"

"You're asking the wrong bird," said the goose. "My friends and I always go south at that time of the year."

Soon a squirrel came by, leaping from tree to tree. "Please, Mr. Squirrel, what is a Christmas tree? And what is Christmas?"

"You're asking the wrong squirrel," he said. "We always sleep through that time of year."

3

Then one stormy day a white dove came to rest on his topmost branch. It landed with a thump, fell off one branch through the next and the next, until the tree pulled his softest branches together to make a thick, green bed that caught and cradled the little white dove.

"Oh, thank you, little tree," said the white dove. "I'm just too, too tired to fly any further. Strong winds blew me away from my home. The beautiful nest I worked so hard on was blown right off the tree, and it's time for me to lay my eggs. Oh, little tree, can you pull your softest branches together and hold them like that as a nest for my eggs?"

For weeks and weeks the little tree struggled to keep his branches close and still as the eggs hatched and three baby doves peeped and cooed. While the busy mother dove was out hunting for seeds, the little tree made an even greater effort and pulled his branches right over them to shelter them from the sun and the rain and hide them from hawks and other dangerous creatures.

The little tree worked so hard helping the white dove raise her children, always pulling his branches over to one side, that he forgot all about growing straight and tall as a Christmas tree should. Gradually he developed a big hump in his trunk.

The farmer walked past and looked disappointed, and he shook his head sadly. He stopped pulling out the weeds around the little tree's trunk. He hardly bothered to spray him for itchy bugs or nibbling caterpillars any more. The little tree felt quite neglected, but he would not give up taking care of the white dove and her children.

The day arrived when the little doves were big enough to learn to fly. They stretched their wings and flapped all the way to the next tree and back. Gradually they began to fly further and further, but they always came back to the little tree at dusk.

One day the mother dove said to the tree, "Oh, little tree, by saving my life and taking care of my children you've grown a big hump in your trunk. The farmer hardly bothers to pull out the weeds around you or spray your branches anymore, and it's all my fault.

"Now it's time for us to fly back to the big tree where I once lived. The people in the house nearby put out seeds every day in the winter for me, as they did for my mother and grandmother before me. It's so hard to find food when the ground is covered in snow, and besides, I'm sure they miss us. But I promise we'll all be back to visit with you in the spring. Tell me, is there anything I can do for you before we go?"

"Please, Mrs. Dove," cried the little tree, "before you go, can you tell me what a Christmas tree is, and what Christmas is? I know that I'll never be a proper Christmas tree now, but I would still like to know what I might have been, and what all the trees I grew up with are going to be."

"Little tree," said the dove, "Christmas is a time when people celebrate the birth of Jesus Christ, who was born to bring peace to the world. Just before Christmas, families bring their children to find a nice, straight Christmas tree. They cut it down and take it home, where it is decorated with coloured lights and shiny ornaments, and they place gifts around it. Grandparents and aunts and uncles and friends all come to admire the tree. Then, when the holiday is over, the lights and ornaments are put away and the poor tree is thrown out, alone, in the snow. By saving me and my children you have grown crooked, but now you are safe."

With this, the white dove and her children flew off.

The snow came, the winds howled, the pond froze. The birds flew south, the squirrels slept, nothing and no one moved on Brown's Christmas Tree Farm.

Then one day, with the snow softly falling, the field was filled with people. Mothers, fathers, children, all laughing and talking, all looking for the perfect tree to take home. Some even looked at the little tree, but when they brushed the snow from his branches and saw the hump on his trunk, they shook their heads and moved on.

But along with the laughter, the thud of axes and the sound of splitting wood filled the air. The little tree stood helpless as one by one all the other trees fell and were dragged away to the waiting cars.

That was the loneliest time of the tree's life. All that long, cold winter he stood alone with nothing to shelter him from the icy winds. When the spring came, no birds stopped by, for one lonely, crooked tree in an empty field was no place to rest on their long journey. Farmer Brown came out with some men, who planted hundreds of baby Christmas trees in rows up and down the field. No one took any notice of the little tree, except to hang their coats on his branches.

One warm and sunny morning, there was a gentle cooing and a flapping of wings. The white dove had kept her promise and had brought her children back to visit.

"Oh, I missed you so much," sobbed the little tree. "I thought that winter had taken you from me. Oh, Mrs. Dove, I'm so alone. They cut down all the friends I grew up with and took them away. No one wanted me because of the hump on my trunk. Nobody was left to shelter me from the icy winds. Farmer Brown planted rows of baby trees, but they're far too young for me to talk to. You told me that a Christmas tree only has coloured lights and shiny ornaments for a short time, but I'd rather bring happiness and laughter to children for those special few days than be lonely and cold all winter by myself. Isn't that what I was made for, to be a symbol of joy and love?"

The white dove and her children comforted the little tree. They stayed with him all day, and flew off with a promise to return soon.

Summer came, and one day Farmer Brown
arrived with some men, some shovels and a
strange machine. They dug and dug and dug all
around the little tree's roots. They wrapped them
in damp sacking, then used the machine to lift
him carefully out of the ground and onto a truck.

It was a long journey lying on his side, with the
sun drying his roots and making him thirsty.
Eventually the truck arrived at a big house, where
a deep hole was waiting in the garden, just the
shape and size of the little tree's roots. They lifted
him carefully from the truck, undid the sacking,
placed him in the hole and filled in the earth
around him. Then they soaked the ground with
cool, fresh water. The little tree sighed and settled
his roots gratefully.

The next day, he looked around at his new home. All kinds of strange flowers grew nearby. The grass was even and green, not tufted with the brown patches that he was used to. But, strangest of all, he was surrounded by the most unusual trees. The little Christmas tree had never seen anything like them. He was positively dwarfed by them! Some grew in clumps, others towered alone to the sky, and some even had flowers on their branches. There wasn't another Christmas tree in sight.

Nevertheless, it was nice to be with trees again, so he plucked up his courage and spoke to one. "Excuse me, sir. I'm a Christmas tree. Who are you?"

"Harrumph," replied the haughty birch. "You're not a real tree. You're just a scrubby little spruce with a crooked trunk and prickly needles. A real tree has silver bark and soft green leaves. You don't belong in this garden." With that, he turned his leaves to the sun and ignored the little tree.

Timidly, the little tree turned his branches up and spoke to the giant behind him. "Excuse me, sir. I just arrived last night. I'm a Christmas tree. Who are you?"

"By my acorns," thundered the proud oak, "real trees grow straight and tall. You're not a real tree. You're just a crooked little nothing."

And so it was with all the others. They wouldn't speak to him because he wasn't tall enough, or straight enough, or wearing the right colour bark. The little Christmas tree was just as lonely as he had been in the empty field. Even the birds ignored him, preferring to perch in the branches of the taller trees.

As summer turned to autumn and nights became cold, all the trees started to change. Their greens turned to golds and browns. Leaves hung limply from branches and then fell to the ground. The giant oak shivered naked in the winter winds. The haughty birch, whose bark was not quite as fine when there were no leaves to hide it, shook in the sleet and rain. The only one who stood green and fresh in the garden was the little Christmas tree.

Even as autumn turned to winter, and the rain turned to snow, the little tree stood proudly green and fresh, with a lacy coat of fluffy white snow on his branches.

One cold day the people of the house came out to the little tree with big boxes full of beautiful things. They hung strings and strings of coloured lights from his branches, and they decorated him from top to bottom with shiny ornaments and bright ribbons.

The little tree stood as tall and proud as he could. He stretched and strained and tried to stand straight and tall. But with his coloured lights glowing and his shiny ornaments glittering, no one seemed to notice that he was little and crooked. People stopped their cars to admire him. The children of the house checked his lights and ornaments daily to make sure that none had blown off.

On Christmas Eve, the people of the house came out, bundled against the cold. People arrived from all around the neighbourhood. Even strangers stopped to join. Softly, sweetly, they sang in harmony.

O holy night, the stars are brightly shining,
This is the night of our dear saviour's birth.

As the last notes died away in the still night, there was a cooing and a whirring of wings. The people looked up and saw, perched on the very tip of the little tree, a beautiful white dove.

The dove remained on top of the tree until the last neighbour had left and the last child had gone to sleep. Then she slipped closer in among the branches and said softly, "Little Christmas tree, you gave me shelter when I was too tired to fly any further. You gave me your softest branches as a nest for my children. In doing this you caused yourself to grow crooked, and you suffered through a long, cold, lonely winter.

"When we parted, you asked me about Christmas trees, and about the meaning of Christmas. Even then, after seeing the fate of all your friends, you wanted to fulfil your destiny.

"Look down, little tree. Look at your branches. See the shiny ornaments, see the bright lights, see the footprints in the snow of all the people who came to admire you. This is your reward. For many years to come, you will stand proudly in this garden, and every Christmas you will be decorated like this and surrounded by love."

The little tree looked down. He saw himself shining in the dark. He saw the footprints in the snow of all the people who had come to share their joy around him. And he felt bigger and taller than any tree that garden had ever seen.

THE LITTLE CROOKED CHRISTMAS TREE

Michael Cutting   Ron Broda

North Winds Press
A Division of Scholastic Canada Ltd.

Scholastic Canada Ltd
123 Newkirk Road, Richmond Hill, Ontario, Canada L4C 3G5

Scholastic Inc.
730 Broadway, New York, NY 10003, USA

Ashton Scholastic Pty Limited
PO Box 579, Gosford, NSW 2250, Australia

Ashton Scholastic Limited
Private Bag 1, Penrose, Auckland, New Zealand

Scholastic Publications Ltd
Holly Walk, Leamington Spa, Warwickshire CV32 4LS England

Photography by William Kuryluk

Canadian Cataloguing in Publication Data

Cutting, Michael
  The little crooked Christmas tree

ISBN 0-590-73652-3

I. Broda, Ron. II. Title.

PS8555.U85L57 1990   jC813'.54   C90-094254-1
PZ7.C88Li 1990

6 5 4 3 2   Printed in Hong Kong   1 2 3 4 5/9